The Twilight Realm

Monsters

Please visit our website, **www.garethstevens.com**. For a free color catalog of all our high-quality books, call toll free 1-800-542-2595 or fax 1-877-542-2596.

Publisher Cataloging Data

Pipe, Jim, 1966-
Monsters / Jim Pipe.
p.   cm. – (The twilight realm)
Includes bibliographical references and index.
Summary: This book examines stories and reported sightings of strange
creatures, from dragons and killer dogs to Bigfoot and the Loch Ness monster.
Contents: Monster myths – In search of Bigfoot – Just a movie? – Big cats
and black dogs – The beast within – Dragon quest – Terrors of the deep – Beneath the city streets – The
Loch Ness riddle – The lost world – Into the unknown – Twilight quiz.
ISBN 978-1-4339-8755-7 (hard bound) – ISBN 978-1-4339-8756-4 (pbk.)
ISBN 978-1-4339-8757-1 (6-pack)
1. Monsters—Juvenile literature   [1. Monsters]   I. Title
2013
001.944—dc23   2012038516

Published in 2013 by
Gareth Stevens Publishing
111 East 14th Street, Suite 349
New York, NY 10003

Produced for Gareth Stevens by Wayland a division of Hachette Children's Books
a Hachette UK company
www.hachette.co.uk

Editor: Paul Manning
Designer: Paul Manning

Picture Credits
t=top; b=bottom
All images © Shutterstock or Dreamstime, except:

7, www.gawker.com; 8, 9, 13t, 15t, 19b, 23, 25 (Conan Doyle), 27t and b, Wikimedia Commons; 10, 11b, 19t,

www.bergoiata.org.

Printed in the United States of America

CPSIA compliance information: Batch CW13GS: For further information contact Gareth Stevens, New York, New York at 1-800-542-2595.

The Twilight Realm
Monsters

Jim Pipe

Gareth Stevens
Publishing

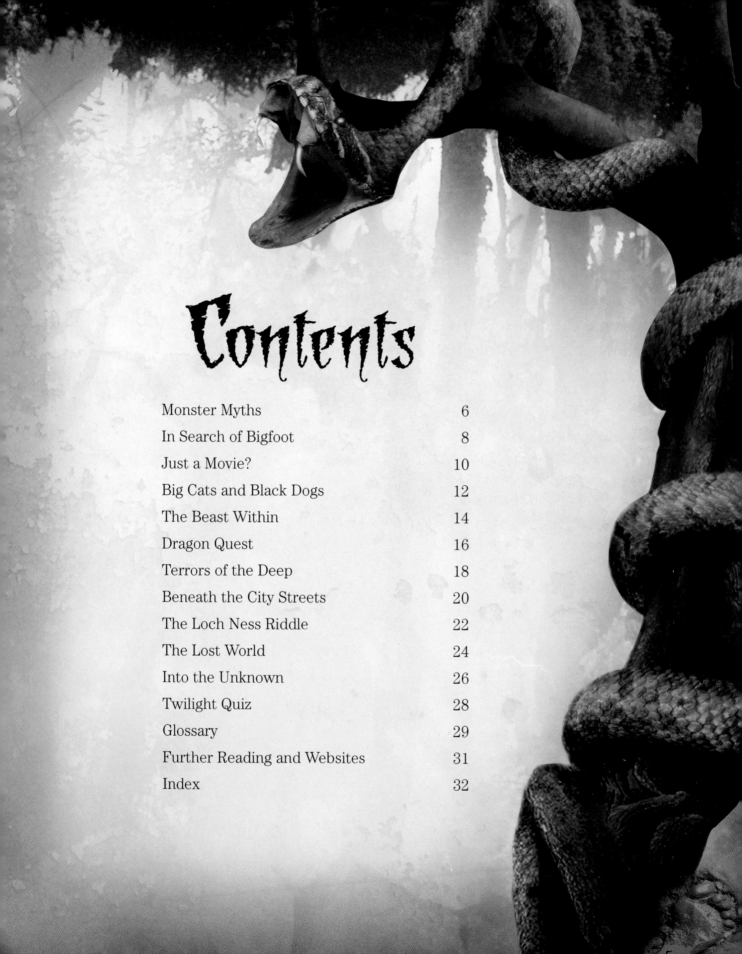

Contents

Monster Myths

Have you ever felt a shudder as you walk the city streets at night, or heard a bloodcurdling howl? If you believe the stories, there are monsters everywhere, from lonely mountaintops to damp city cellars…

▼ *"Mothman" was the name given to a hideous winged creature sighted many times in West Virginia, during the mid 1960s. But was it a monster or simply a great horned owl?*

Today, we look to science to explain frightening natural phenomena such as thunderstorms and lightning. In the past, people relied on myths to explain the world around them. So a whirlpool might be caused by a sea monster sucking sailors into its gaping mouth. Other monster myths came from dangers such as deadly animal predators or invading tribes. Viking warriors wore wolf and bearskins to scare their enemies, and this may be why people started to tell stories about werewolves.

Monster, Cryptid, or Hoax?

Many of the monsters in this book are "cryptids," puzzling animals whose existence is hard to prove. Some are big cats or alligators living in unexpected places. Others may be survivors from ancient times or monstrous relatives of creatures that are fairly common.

▲ In 2008, this bizarre creature, christened the "Rhode Island Monster," was washed ashore on a beach near Montauk, New York. Was it the result of a horrific experiment at a nearby animal lab, a badly rotted body of a raccoon, or just an elaborate hoax?

Some monsters may have been made up by local people playing a joke on visitors. For example, the Aboriginal peoples in Australia told stories about the Yowie, a tall, hairy creature with long fangs, to keep white settlers away from sacred Aboriginal sites.

So much for mythical explanations. But what about all the weird and wonderful creatures sighted in the past 100 years? Many have been photographed or recorded, while strange bones or other remains have been found that are unlike any living animal.

▼ Monsters are often found in wild, lonely places like the Himalayas of Asia, home to the legendary ape-man known as the Yeti.

Skeptics say stories of sea beasts or giant ape-men are just tall tales. There's no doubt that many of these monsters are shy. But ignoring their existence won't keep them from snatching unwary victims…

"Though humans have shared the planet with millions of other creatures for thousands of years, we know surprisingly little about our neighbours. We've discovered just ten percent of all living things on this planet."

From the 2010 Cryptozoological Report

In Search of Bigfoot

A forest ranger is trekking through a remote forest when he glimpses a gigantic ape lumbering through the trees. Could the monster be a survivor from the Stone Age?

Shaggy, ape-like creatures have been seen from Africa to the Himalayas. In 1951, British climber Eric Shipton photographed giant footprints in the snow while mountaineering in Nepal. A few years later, Sir Edmund Hillary, the first man to climb Everest, brought back a skin sample of what he thought was a Yeti. In 1924, lumberjack Albert Ostman claimed that he had been abducted by a whole family of gigantic apes while on a camping trip in the remote forests of British Columbia.

► In Asia, the giant ape monster is known as the Yeti or the Abominable Snowman, while in North America it is called Bigfoot or Sasquatch.

Caught on Camera

Giant, ape-like creatures have often been spotted in North America, but rarely caught on camera. The best-known filmed sighting was by two amateur cryptid hunters, Roger Patterson and Bob Gimlin. In 1977, they managed to shoot a few seconds of film of a tall, hairy creature looking back at the camera before vanishing into the woods near Eureka, California.

Some claimed it was just a prankster in a monkey suit. Others pointed out that the creature's giant strides and springy way of walking were very unhuman. Patterson and Gimlin always denied it was a hoax, and firmly maintained the creature they saw was real.

▲ So far, no one has managed to capture a Yeti or Bigfoot. Until they do, most scientists remain skeptical about whether the ape-men really exist.

► Giant apes certainly did once exist. These huge jaws belong to Gigantopithecus, a nearly 10-foot-tall ape that lived about 1 million to 300,000 years ago. But do any still survive?

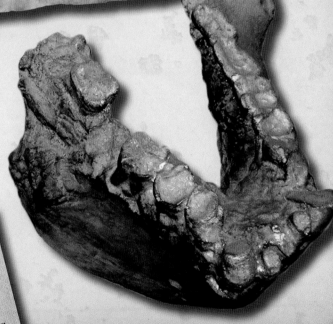

"What really made my flesh creep... was that where we had to jump crevasses, you could see clearly where the creature had dug its toes in."

Eric Shipton, mountaineer, describing Yeti tracks in the snows of Nepal

9

Just a Movie?

It's in our nature to fear the unknown, whether it's horrifying beasts living in remote lands or gruesome creatures created by scientific experiments gone wrong.

Over the years, moviemakers have scared audiences with all sorts of imaginary horrors, from Frankenstein's monster to King Kong. Is there any truth to these terrifying tales?

Scientists are already able to create weird animals by mixing genes from different species. In the 1990s, they created a "geep," a half-sheep, half-goat mix. Other scientists are finding new ways to fight disease by injecting human cells into sheep's brains. Such developments create new imaginative possibilities for storytellers. What if a human mind somehow got trapped inside a sheep's head?

◄ In Mary Shelley's famous novel Frankenstein (1818), a scientist stitches together body parts, then brings them to life with a giant surge of electricity. But he is unable to control the awesome monster he has created.

We've all heard of those monster beasts, the dinosaurs. Most died out 65 million years ago, but descendants of some of these ancient giants survived, like the 20-foot saltwater crocodiles found in Australia.

In spite of satellites and Google Earth, there are still vast, unexplored regions in the world, and all sorts of strange creatures could be lurking there. In 1938, South African fishermen caught a 6.5-foot fish with bulging eyes and thick scales. It was a coelacanth, a creature thought to have died out millions of years ago!

▲ In the story of King Kong, a film crew discovers a giant ape on the mysterious Skull Island. We're still finding large unknown creatures, like the new species of giant 13-foot anaconda snake (above), first discovered in Bolivia in 2002.

"Between 1999 and 2009, one new plant or animal species was discovered every three days, including 637 plants, 257 fish, 216 amphibians, 55 reptiles, 16 birds, and 39 mammals."

from a World Wildlife Fund report, 2010

Outer space could be full of scary monsters, too. In the film *Alien* (1979), hideous space monsters lay their eggs inside human bodies. In *Predator* (1987), an alien armed with hi-tech weapons hunts humans for sport.

Maybe in the distant future, those nightmarish stories could become a reality. Suppose a microscopic lifeform hitched a ride on a comet, landed on Earth, and took over our bodies, turning *us* into monsters!

Big Cats and Black Dogs

Imagine walking across a lonely moor, when out of the mists bounds a giant, shaggy dog with huge, saucerlike eyes and monstrous, slavering jaws. Nicknamed "Black Shuck" by the locals, it's as big as a small horse!

Strange beasts have been spotted in remote areas of Britain for centuries. In the early 1990s, many people claimed to have spotted big cats such as the notorious "Beast of Bodmin." In 1995, a 14-year-old boy discovered a skull with large fangs on Bodmin Moor in Cornwall. Scientists at London's Natural History Museum confirmed it was that of a leopard. Inside were cockroach eggs from the tropics, proving the skull was a hoax. But the sightings go on!

▼ *Black, pantherlike creatures have been seen in the wilds of Scotland, as well as on the desolate moors of Devon and Cornwall in southern England.*

The Hound of the Baskervilles

Fearsome black dogs have been known to walk alongside lonely travelers without harming them at all – but you wouldn't want to take any chances with the ferocious beast in Arthur Conan Doyle's novel *The Hound of the Baskervilles*, published in 1901.

Sherlock Holmes is called to investigate after Sir Charles Baskerville is found dead of a heart attack, with giant pawprints near his body. Could this be the phantom hound that has cursed the Baskerville family for centuries? Holmes's skillful detective work uncovers a plot to steal the Baskerville fortune by scaring the family to death with a terrifying ghostly hound that roams the moors at night.

► When Sherlock Holmes finally meets the monstrous Hound of the Baskervilles face-to-face, he realizes it's just a very large dog covered in special paint that makes it glow in the dark.

"As the light faded, I could hear something growling and hissing nearby. Suddenly there was a flash of black as a giant panther leapt up onto a large rock. Raising its head, it let out a bloodcurdling howl and I could feel my legs go weak with fright…"

An eyewitness describes an encounter with the so-called "Beast of Bodmin"

The Beast Within

A full moon glows in the sky above. A man screams in pain. Bones crack, muscles grow. Thick hair sprouts, claws erupt from toes and fingers, and fangs burst from his mouth. With a terrifying howl, man has become werewolf!

▼ Tales of werewolves are told all over the world, and appear in Viking, Roman, and ancient Greek legends. In South America, the local wolfman is called a lobizón. The Navajo people of the southwestern United States call werewolves "skin-walkers."

"They were like wolves, but their faces were small and long... In some villages they devoured more than 100 people... These monsters entered houses and... climbed onto terraces in the night, and stole children from their beds."

An account of werewolves in Iraq by Denys of Tell-Mahre, a Syrian scribe writing around AD 770

The Curse of the Werewolf

In medieval times, people believed that anyone bitten by a werewolf, or who ate wolf flesh, became a werewolf, too. Today, it's thought that the "werewolf's curse" could be a virus that transforms the victims' bodies and turns them into crazed monsters.

In the movies, only a silver bullet can kill a werewolf. But according to other sources, most weapons will do the job – if you can get close enough! In the 17th century, church leaders recommended hacking off a werewolf's head with a double-edged sword or stabbing it between the eyebrows with a pitchfork.

▲ Watch out, some werewolves hunt in packs! One summer's evening in 1439, a pack of werewolves was reported to have run silently through the streets of Paris and devoured 14 people in a single night!

It's said that by day, werewolves are much like other folk, save for a few telltale signs, such as hairy palms, thick eyebrows that meet in the middle, and small, slightly pointed ears. But when the moon is full, they turn into vicious wolflike creatures that tear the throats out of their victims, then gorge on their flesh.

Is it just a myth? In 16th-century Europe, some 30,000 people were executed for being werewolves. During the 1760s, the "Beast of Gévaudan" killed 40 people and injured many others in south-central France. After a very large wolf was caught and killed, the attacks came to an end. However, local people still claimed they'd seen a werewolf with jaws as big as a lion's…

Dragon Quest

Dragons are our worst nightmare: massive, flying predators with vicious talons and a mouth stuffed with razor-sharp teeth. Oh yes, and they breathe fire, too!

▲ *If you ever come across two dragons fighting (they're very bad-tempered), it's probably best to stand well back and leave them to it.*

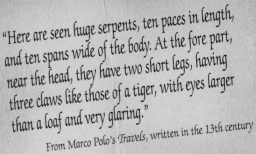

Dragon Lore

In myths and legends, most dragons live alone and spend their days sleeping in hidden caves where they hoard their treasure. But once roused, they're deadly predators. On the hunt, they swoop low over the ground, snatching prey with their gaping jaws or talons. After a large meal, a dragon can sleep for several months without needing to feed again.

Most dragons breathe long jets of fire, but a hairy French dragon known as a Peluda uses its acidic breath or the poisonous stingers on its body to kill its victims.

▲ *According to legend, if dragons' teeth are planted in the ground, they will grow into fully armed warriors.*

Medieval scholars tell of dragons over 30 feet (10 m) long, with the body of a huge lizard; tough, scaly skin; four legs with giant talons; a long tail; enormous bat-like wings; and a pair of horns sprouting from their head. Could these monsters be related to dinosaurs? It's hard to know.

In tales of old, dragons were quickly tracked down and killed by brave knights in shining armor. Today's dragon hunters are more wary.

Dragons are said to have sharp eyes and a keen sense of smell, so you need to keep your wits about you. If you suspect there's a dragon's lair in your area, look for burn marks at the cave entrance, caused by the dragon's fiery breath. Other clues include traces of scaly skin and a cave floor littered with bones. If you find a nest of dragon eggs, leave them alone. You *don't* want a furious mother dragon on your tail!

Terrors of the Deep

For centuries, seafarers across the globe have warned of giant monsters lurking deep in the oceans. Should we believe them?

Terrifying sea creatures have often been spotted by passing ships. In 1905, two British scientists were traveling on the steamship *Valhalla* off the coast of Brazil when they saw a giant head rise out of the water, with a neck as thick as a man's body. The monster appeared again the next evening, this time swimming past the ship at great speed. Several other witnesses on board described a long sea serpent with a "head like a horse."

◄ Are sea monsters ancient giants? Megalodon, a 52-foot (16 m) shark that lived 16 million years ago, would have weighed 30 times more than this Great White.

► In 1755, Bishop Pontopiddan of Bergen, Norway, wrote that "floating islands" that appeared on the sea then suddenly disappeared were probably a giant sea monster called the Kraken coming to the surface.

Norwegian sailors feared a gigantic sea monster known as the Kraken. Its tentacles could drag a whole ship under the waves, creating a whirlpool that sucked down any sailors who escaped its grasp.

Few believed the stories. Then, in the 1940s, a huge squid was seen swimming alongside a ship. Today, deep-sea scientists are exploring many of the deepest parts of the ocean for the first time. What they will find? In recent years, sonar devices have picked up a mysterious sound made by an animal much too large to be a whale. Could this be a Kraken skulking in the depths?

"We were sailing off the coast of south-west Africa when two giant arms suddenly rose out of the water, snatched three of my crew and dragged them below the waves. We sank five harpoons into the monster before it was finished."

18th-century Danish sea captain Jean Magnus Dens

▲ Sea serpents, like the monstrous leviathan shown in this engraving by Gustave Doré, don't just exist in stories. In 1996, US marines caught a giant oar fish that was 23 feet (7 m) long. Its body was a metallic silver, with a bright red stripe running along its length.

19

Beneath the City Streets

Did you know that there are giant rats swarming under the streets of London, or that enormous alligators thrive in the sewers of New York City? Well, that's what they say...

▼ Could an alligator really survive in a sewer? Not according to the experts. If the polluted water didn't kill it, they argue, freezing winter temperatures probably would.

Monster Vermin

A Victorian tale told of ferocious "black pigs" living in the sewers of North London and feeding on the garbage washed into them. In recent times, the story has been changed: now they're giant rats infesting our underground tunnels.

There's a grain of truth in this. Fattened by leftover junk food, a new breed of bigger, bolder rat has been spotted in some of our cities. This super rat can nibble through concrete, leap almost 3 feet (1 m) in the air, and is increasingly unaffected by rat poison.

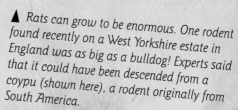

▲ Rats can grow to be enormous. One rodent found recently on a West Yorkshire estate in England was as big as a bulldog! Experts said that it could have been descended from a coypu (shown here), a rodent originally from South America.

Back in the 1970s, there was a craze among New Yorkers vacationing in Florida for bringing back baby alligators for their children to raise as pets. Once the little gators outlived their cuteness, their owners flushed them down the toilet.

According to popular legend, some of these unwanted pets managed to survive and breed in the New York City sewer system. Growing fat on the city's waste, the alligators developed into a monstrous new breed. They're still there today, attacking anyone who dares to venture into their dark underground realm…

Believe it or not, an 8-foot (2.5 m) alligator was caught at the bottom of a New York drain in 1935, and abandoned pets are still turning up on the city streets. In 2006, a 3-foot (1 m) caiman lizard snapped and hissed at police officers before it was caught outside a Brooklyn apartment building.

Could monstrous creatures be living in the sewers under your streets?
- Read your local paper and look for reports of missing sewage workers.
- Are there unusual pawprints in your garden?
- Can you hear weird sounds coming from manholes or from under the ground?

The Loch Ness Riddle

In 1951, Lachlan Stuart was heading out early one morning to milk his cows on the banks of Loch Ness, in the Scottish Highlands, when he saw a strange rippling in the waters. Three humps rose out of the lake, then moved in line with the shore!

Over the centuries, many others claim to have caught a glimpse of the Loch Ness monster. More recently, people also claimed to have photographed and filmed "Nessie," but the creature remains as mysterious as ever. For the murky waters of Loch Ness are over 650 feet (200 m) deep in parts – the perfect place for a prehistoric monster to stay hidden from meddling humans!

▲ Some people believe the Loch Ness monster is a plesiosaur, a type of ancient four-flippered lizard left over from the time of the dinosaurs. Others argue that there aren't enough fish in the loch to feed such a massive creature.

"The creature, a dragon or prehistoric animal, was carrying a small lamb or animal of some kind… it had a long neck which moved up and down… and the body was fairly big, with a high back."

A sighting of the Loch Ness monster by Mr. and Mrs. George Spicer in 1933

The first known sighting of Nessie was by the Irish saint Columba, who saw the monster rise to the surface of the lake "with a great roar and open mouth" in the 6th century. The saint ordered the beast back below the waters, and it obeyed!

The Nessie story really took off after sightings in 1933 and in 1934, when a London surgeon, Dr. Robert Wilson, took what was thought to be the first photo of the monster. This showed a small-headed creature with a long, arching neck and a bulky body creating unconvincingly small ripples in the water. In 1994, the photograph was declared a fake. It turned out that the monster Wilson had snapped was nothing more than a toy submarine with a sculpted head made of plastic wood!

Hoaxes aside, we'll probably never know for sure if the Loch Ness monster really exists. But many people have a secret affection for Nessie (she even has her own fan club), and would like the stories to be true!

▼ Another possible candidate for the Loch Ness monster is dolichorhynchops, a type of seagoing prehistoric reptile.

Now You See Her, Now You Don't

Over the past 70 years, several photographs have been taken of the Loch Ness monster, some more convincing than others, but none providing conclusive proof.

- In April 1960, flight engineer Tim Dinsdale filmed a hump moving across the loch at about 6 miles (11 km) per hour.

- In 1969, the six-man submarine *Pisces* searched the loch with little success, though it did find a large underwater cavern that could be the monster's lair.

- In 1972, another submarine snapped what looked very much like a huge flipper under the water.

- In 1987, scientists using sonar equipment picked up movements of a giant shape under the water. Could this have been Nessie? But what animal could live for 1,400 years?

The Lost World

Mapmakers once marked the edges of the known world with drawings of sea serpents, dragons, and other monsters. Even today, unexplored lands could be inhabited by strange beasts.

Several writers have tried to imagine these lost worlds. In Edgar Rice Burroughs' *The Land That Time Forgot* (1924), the writer describes a lost island in the middle of the South Pacific that is home to winged, humanlike creatures, dinosaurs, ferocious beasts of prey, and huge reptiles. This motley band of monsters terrorize the human adventurers who find themselves stranded on the island.

► *Could there be a lost underground kingdom? In Jules Verne's* Journey to the Center of the Earth *(1864), giant reptiles live under Earth's crust, beside a vast underground sea.*

▶ Millions of years ago, winged creatures called pterodactyls were the earliest reptiles to develop the ability to fly.

Burroughs borrowed this idea from Arthur Conan Doyle's novel *The Lost World*. Written in 1912, it told the story of an expedition to a high plateau above the Amazon jungle of South America, where dinosaurs and other extinct creatures still survived.

Such ideas are not that far-fetched. There are still places in the world that have not been seen by human eyes, so who knows what might be out there? In 2006, an international team of scientists found a "lost world" in a remote Indonesian jungle that was home to dozens of undiscovered animal and plant species.

The idea of a forgotten animal kingdom was given a new twist in the film *Jurassic Park* (1993), in which cloned dinosaurs go on the rampage in a safari park. Again, this is not a million miles from reality. Thanks to genetic engineering, we may soon be able to bring long-dead animals back to life, such as the woolly mammoth, extinct for over 10,000 years.

▲ In The Lost World by Arthur Conan Doyle (1859–1930), a group of Victorian adventurers face rampaging horned dinosaurs, pterodactyls, and many other prehistoric predators.

"Suddenly out of the darkness, out of the night, there swooped something with a swish like an aeroplane... I had a momentary vision of a long, snake-like neck, a fierce, red, greedy eye, and a great snapping beak, filled, to my amazement, with little, gleaming teeth."

description of a pterodactyl from The Lost World by Arthur Conan Doyle

Into the Unknown

How intrepid are you? Would you hack your way through unexplored jungle, or trek across vast deserts in search of unseen monsters?

Serious monster hunters study the science of "hidden" animals, known as cryptozoology. If this sounds like the job for you, you'll need a variety of skills. A knowledge of local languages and customs is vital, along with tracking skills and an ability to survive and find your way in the wilderness. If you get lucky and actually corner an unknown creature, you'll also need to be handy with a dart gun and tranquilizers to capture the beast alive. All set? Then here's a couple of missing monsters to hunt down…

◀ *Canoeing across a remote mountain lake is fine until you are attacked by a huge, fast moving monster!*

There are mythical monsters all over the world waiting to be discovered. Visit your local library and see what can you find out about:
• The thunderbird of the Arizona desert
• The fiery salamander of India
• The merfolk of the northern seas

Mokele-Mbembe

Ever since the first explorers returned from Africa, there have been rumors of a monster living in the swampy jungles of the Congo basin. As big as an elephant, it is said to have smooth, brown skin, a long neck, a small head (like a plant-eating dinosaur), a long tail, and clawed feet. Some believe this monster, known as mokele-mbembe, is a living fossil surviving from prehistoric times.

The Mongolian Death Worm

Mongolian folklore describes a giant death worm that lives underground for most of the year except for the rainy season. This hideous creature is described as a fat, bright-red worm about 3 feet (1 m) long that spits out a deadly yellow poison. In 2005, a British expedition went deep into the Gobi desert to look for the worm, known locally as the olgoi-khorkhoi, but failed to find it. Would YOU like to join the search?

The Ogopogo

Another good place to make your mark as a monster hunter is Lake Okanagan in Canada. This is said to be inhabited by the Ogopogo, which was spotted by a large group of witnesses in 1926.

▲ An 1872 engraving of the Ogopogo. Twelve years earlier, a local man was supposedly dragged under the water by the beast.

In 1989, father and son Clem and Ken Chaplin claimed to have seen the creature swimming in the lake and making a splash with a flick of its giant tail. British cryptozoologist Karl Shuker has suggested the Ogopogo could be a basilosaurus, an ancient serpent-like whale that grew up to 60 feet (18 m) long!

► Basilosaurus skeletons were first discovered in the southern United States. In some parts of the country they are so common that they are used as furniture.

Twilight Quiz

1. An alligator has been sighted in the sewers below your town. How should you tackle it?

   a Back the beast into a corner by shouting down the nearest manhole: "Be very, very afraid – alligator handbags are back in fashion!"

   b Interview witnesses carefully (it could be a hoax) before carrying out an armed search of the area where the creature was sighted.

   c What's the rush? Check out video footage of the area before taking any unnecessary risks.

2. You're asked to coordinate a new hunt for the Loch Ness monster. Should you:

   a Hire an attack submarine to make Nessie history once and for all?

   b Use a combination of underwater sonar devices and video cameras to make a sweep of the entire Loch?

   c Fling a few tins of tuna into the water to lure the monster to the surface, then sit back and wait?

3. You're hunting down a dinosaur-like creature in a remote jungle valley. What's your first step?

   a Set fire to the jungle. You'll either flush the creature out or be eating roast dino for dinner.

   b Ask the locals the best place to start your search, then assemble a first-rate team of scientists, trackers, and helicopter crews.

   c Relax. If there's anything big in there, Google Earth will have picked it up.

4. There are reports of werewolves in your neighbourhood. Should you:

   a Load up with silver bullets and round up anyone with bushy eyebrows or hairy palms? Better safe than sorry.

   b Wait until the moon is full, then lay a trap for the werewolf using the strongest nets you can find? If you catch one, keep far away until dawn!

   c Ask the neighbors if anybody's lost a pet recently?

5. You're high in the Himalayas when you come face-to-face with a Yeti. What next?

   a Howl as loudly as you can. With any luck, you'll set off an avalanche that'll bury the monster.

   b Remember these creatures are very shy. Stay calm, avoid sudden movements, and try to get some good photos and video footage.

   c Hop on your sled and skedaddle back down the mountain as fast as you can. This is one crazy story you have to tell your friends!

CHECK YOUR SCORE

Mostly 'a's Full marks for enthusiasm, but you'd probably add a few more creatures to the extinct list!

Mostly 'b's Well done! You've got the right combination of brains, bravery, and patience.

Mostly 'c's Hmm. Not sure you'd hang around long enough to confirm a sighting of anything!

Glossary

abduct to kidnap or carry off

Aboriginal describing the earliest
known inhabitants of Australia

acidic sharp, bitter-tasting;
able to dissolve metals

clone to copy a living creature or
organism by genetic engineering

crevasse a deep, narrow
crack in a sheet of ice

cryptid a creature that does not
belong to any known species
and may or may not exist

cryptozoology the study of cryptids

desolate lonely, remote

devour to eat greedily, like an animal

extinct no longer in existence

(folk)lore stories, customs, and traditions

fossilized turned to stone

gene the biological blueprint inside our
bodies that we inherit from our parents,
and that makes us what we are

genetic engineering changing plants
and animals by modifying their genes

gorge to feast upon

gruesome horrible, revolting

hoard to collect and keep safe,
e.g. gold or treasure

hoax a deliberate attempt to
trick or fool people

lair the home of an animal or
creature such as a dragon

legend a traditional story that may or
may not be based on real events

loch a Scottish word for "lake"

lumberjack a woodcutter or forester

manhole a covered opening
over a drain or sewer

Glossary (continued)

medieval belonging to the Middle Ages, the period roughly from the 5th to the 15th centuries

motley mixed, varied

myth a belief that may not be true; an ancient or traditional story

pitchfork a tool with two sharp prongs

plateau an area of flat, high ground

prankster someone who plays tricks on people

predator an animal that hunts other creatures for food

reptile a cold-blooded animal such as a snake or lizard

rodent a type of mammal such as a mouse or rat

scholar a learned person

sewer an underground drain

skeptic someone who questions other people's beliefs or opinions

slavering slobbering; dripping saliva

sonar equipment for locating and tracking objects underwater

Stone Age the prehistoric period when people used tools and weapons made of stone

talon a sharp claw, e.g. of a bird of prey

tropics the regions immediately north and south of the Equator

unwary unsuspecting or careless

vermin animals that live on food waste, such as rats, mice, and cockroaches

wary careful

Further Reading and Websites

Further Reading

In Search of Sasquatch, Kelly Milner Halls (Houghton Mifflin Harcourt)

The Mystery of the Loch Ness Monster, Holly Wallace (Can Science Solve…? series, Heinemann)

Sea Monsters: A Prehistoric Adventure, Mose Richards (National Geographic Society)

Werewolves, Jim Pipe (Tales of Horror series, Ticktock Media Ltd.)

Encyclopedia Horrifica: The Terrifying TRUTH! About Vampires, Ghosts, Monsters and More, Joshua Gee (Scholastic Books)

The Unexplained: Encounters with Ghosts, Monsters and Aliens, Jim Pipe (Ticktock Media Ltd.)

An Illustrated Guide to Mythical Creatures, Anita Ganeri and David West (Bookhouse)

Websites

www.livingsasquatch.com
A fun site that allows you to make your own Sasquatch movie.

www.nessie.co.uk
Website dedicated to the Loch Ness monster, with pictures and a timeline of sightings.

www.newanimal.org
Find out about monster hunting and all sorts of weird and wonderful cryptids.

http://sd4kids.skepdic.com/monsters.htm/
An explanation of what scientists say about monsters.

http://www.skeptiseum.org/index.php?id=none&cat=cryptozoology/
A museum on the web with pictures and descriptions of things from around the world that are connected to a belief in monsters.

http://www.unmuseum.org/lostw.htm/
At this "museum of unnatural mystery" on the web, you can find out about monsters on land and at sea.

Index